Going Somewhere Soon

Volume 3: Collected Stories & Drawings of Brian Andreas

StoryPeople
Decorah

ISBN 0-9642660-2-4

The people in this book, if at one time real, are now entirely fictitious, having been subjected to a combination of a selective memory and a fertile imagination. Any resemblance to real people you might know, even if they are the author's relatives, is entirely coincidental, and is a reminder that you are imagining the incidents in this book as much as the author is.

StoryPeople
P.O. Box 7
Decorah, IA 52101
USA
563.382.8060
563.382.0263 FAX
800.476.7178

storypeople@storypeople.com
www.storypeople.com

First Edition: *March, 1995*
Second Edition: *March, 2004*

Produced by West Coast Print Center, Oakland, California
on 30% tree-free kenaf / 70% recycled, chlorine-free archival text paper

To my sons, David Quinn and Matthew Shea, for their promise and wonder, and for all the wild places we've been, and to my beloved Ellen, forever and always, for every late night conversation and dance, and for patiently teaching me every day the secrets of an open heart.

Other books by Brian Andreas available
from StoryPeople Press:

Mostly True
Still Mostly True
Strange Dreams
Hearing Voices
Trusting Soul
Story People
Traveling Light

Cover Art: Brian Andreas
Back photo: David Cavagnaro

Going Somewhere Soon

Introduction

This is the last book of the *Mostly True* trilogy. There's been so much that's happened since I began: we've gone from babies to boys, and moved from the West Coast back to a small town in Iowa. All the while, I've travelled around the country telling stories and meeting many of you.

And I've had letters. Beautiful and warm and filled with stories. The simple stories you see here have touched people in ways I can only begin to understand. Last holiday season, I was sitting at my desk when a FAX came in. In part it read, "your gift to the world became your gift to me. It came just in time to remind me I'm not dead." *To remind me I'm not dead.* I wondered once how I would describe to my boys what it was like to be alive at the end of the Twentieth Century. Your letters are a great part of the answer I will give them someday. They have meant a lot to me, and I thank you for every one.

Many of you have asked where the stories come from. I don't have an answer for that. All I know is that the stories we love are about ourselves. The stories we tell about our children, the family myths from our grandmothers and grandfathers, even the eerie fables that leap at us from the Enquirer in the grocery store, are all stories about ourselves. Our lives can be intricate puzzles, filled with remembering and forgetting, all the pieces scattered seemingly at random. Stories are the one guide I've found to be true. They are the signs pointing the way across our inner landscape.

I offer the stories here in the same spirit they came to me, as gifts of laughter and love and possibility. Read them. Listen to their voices inside yourself. Listen for what feels right. The stories in this book, and the ones before it, are a set of maps of inner space. When you find the right story, it will guide you unerringly. I don't know why or how this works, but I know that it does. Many people have told me these stories touch places they have forgotten or never known. They can be the beginning of a great journey, for there are stories within you that will dwarf these small offerings with their wonder and anguish and forgotten power...

With love,

14 February 1995

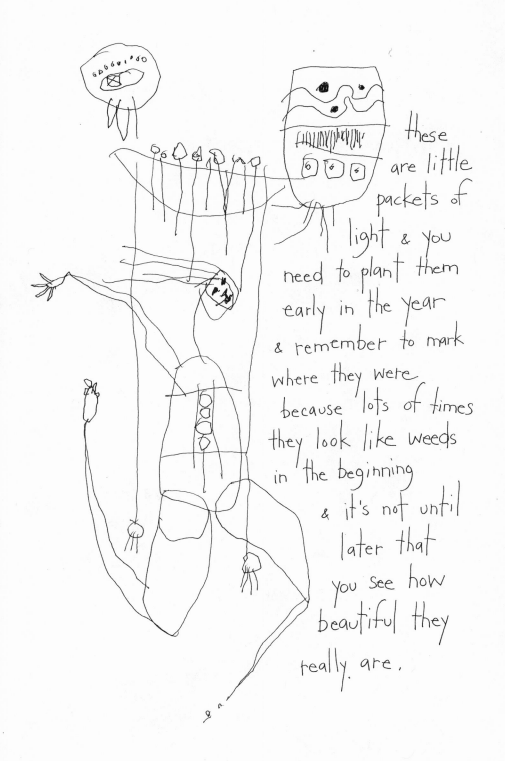

these
are little
packets of
light & you
need to plant them
early in the year
& remember to mark
where they were
because lots of times
they look like weeds
in the beginning
& it's not until
later that
you see how
beautiful they
really are.

My great · grandmother sent
us out to pick raspberries
in her garden while she
watched the first moon
walk on tv. You'll have
plenty of time to see things
like that, she said, but
those raspberries were
carried overland by your
great · great · grandfather.
She was very wise. I see
pictures of the moonwalk
all the time, but all I have
left from him is the memory
of those sun · warmed
raspberries.

Raspberry Patch

I've always liked living in the past best, she said.

It takes less money than I make now.

Living in the Past

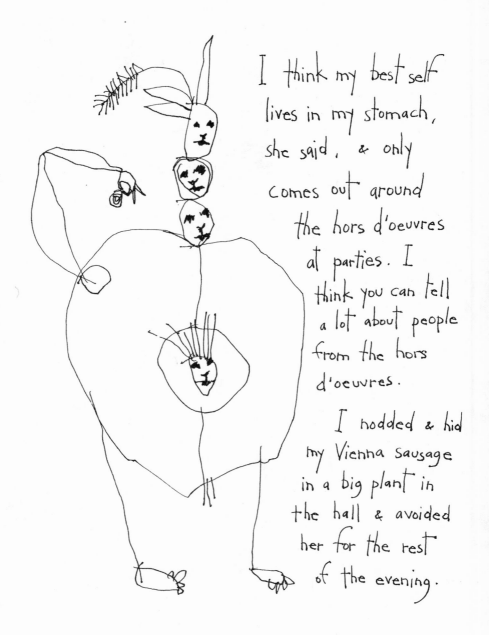

I think my best self lives in my stomach, she said, & only comes out around the hors d'oeuvres at parties. I think you can tell a lot about people from the hors d'oeuvres.

I nodded & hid my Vienna sausage in a big plant in the hall & avoided her for the rest of the evening.

Hors D'Oeuvres

I don't
really have
any secrets,
she told
me once.
I just
forget
a lot of
stuff.

Forgetful

She moved with the grace of
a cat & her tongue licked at
the corner of her lips & I'm
sure she would have helped
me if I could have said I
am just a child & don't know
what to do, but I was just
a child & didn't know how to
tell her about those new &
raw places in my heart, so
she stood there in the dim
light with her hair like a cloud
of perfume around her face &
neither of us spoke & now I
wish I could go back & hold
her & say someday we will
laugh & ache about this.

New Places

He told me once that he never planned
to settle down. It's not that I'm afraid
of commitment, he
said, I just
hate to mow.

Hate to Mow

My great-aunt Clara told us
once about the time she was
one of the wise men in the
church play & when it came to

her part she said we're here
bearing frankincense, gold & myrrh,
heavy on the frankincense because
of that camel smell & after that her
father always called it the story of
the Two Wise Men & that other guy
& we laughed so hard we had to pee.

I thought, I'll
remove my head
for a while & it
went fine except
most people didn't

know where to
look when we
were having a
conversation.

I try not to collect too much because having stuff takes more time than you think.

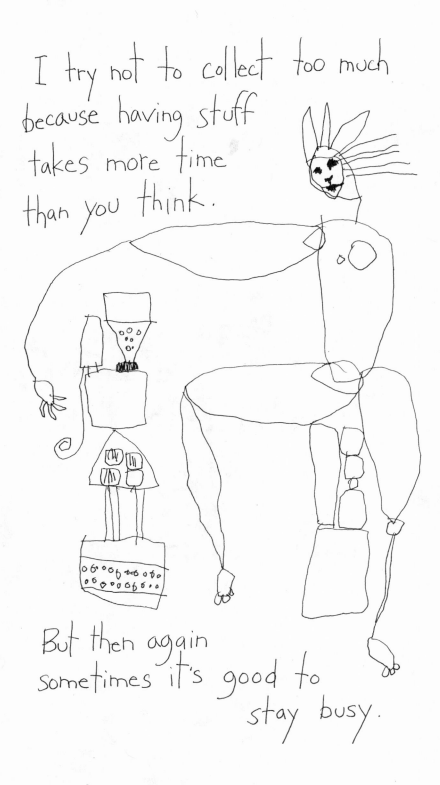

But then again sometimes it's good to stay busy.

He told me that once
he forgot himself & his
heart opened up like a
door with a loose latch
& everything fell out &
he tried for days to put
it all back in the proper
order, but finally he
gave up & left it there
in a pile & loved
everything equally.

Open Heart

How old do you have
to be to die? he said
& I said I didn't
think anybody was
ever old enough

    & that made sense
    to him since he
    was still new to
    the world &
    remembered how
    forever had been.

Forever

When I was young
I always wanted to go exploring in a cave
and when I got older I finally did &
it was dark everywhere & there were
strange sounds like your stomach after a
big meal & I
couldn't wait
to get out.
I figured
out later

that I
mainly liked to
go exploring caves in
my mind where I could
be comfortable & not get dirty & cold. If you read
too much National Geographic when you're young
it's hard to adjust to the real world.

Sometimes I think I'm going to end up all alone in a cold apartment living on cat food from a can

MEOW!
MEOW!

but I guess that's not so bad since I'm a cat after all

Old Cat

My great·aunt told
me once to remember
that old people need
bananas.

I remember.
Someday I will
tell my sons.

he used to make model balloons & send them
off to Macy's with a note that they could
use them free of charge   for
their parades.

After
Macy's
filed for
bankruptcy

he just
shook
his head.

A better
balloon could've turned that whole
              situation around, he
                        said.

Every summer we had a circus
& I always got to be the fortune
teller. All the girls wanted to
know if they'd have babies & all
the boys wanted to find out about
the Cubs.

We had one neighbor who'd been
in the hospital who asked me if
I could tell her when she was
going to die & I didn't know
what to say so I told her not
before her time & then she grabbed
my arm & said I was a good boy
but that's not what the doctors
said & there I was looking in
the crystal ball wishing I had
more Gypsy & less Norwegian.

My great uncle shot
& killed his own
brother for disturbing
the peace & I wonder
if anyone ever tried
to quiet his deep deep
sorrow. Duty isn't
consolation enough.

I watched the pellet leave
the gun. It was like a
big black fly & it
landed on the blackbird's
wing & suddenly there

was
a
single
drop of bright
bright red & the
voices of the
world seemed
farther away & I
knew I could never
do that again

the
sounds of the
other birds stopped
for a moment as
its song flew out to all the corners of the world
& I hoped that someday I would be remembered
that way

One summer we
visited my grandparents,
I remember we went
to a dance in the
country. The band
was loud & enthusiastic
& there were so many
people my glasses
got steamed up.
After a while,
the band
stopped for
a drink

& my ears were still
ringing & I looked up &
there were strings of white
lights scattered like stars
all over the ceiling & I
wondered if it was this bright out
in space where there were no people

& then the band started playing another polka
& the quiet slipped out to the front porch
with all the other old guys.

The first time
I played golf,
I had the most
fun throwing
bread to the
goldfish in the
pro shop. It
made as much
sense as anything
else.

I used to eat
popcorn for
every meal,

she told me
once. It made
me feel like

I was — in
the
movies
& my
life

would turn
out happy
in the end.
Did it work?
I said.

I don't know, she said,
but I like to think the
roughage counts for something.

There are times
I think I'm doing
things on principle,
but mostly I just
do what feels
good.

But that's a
principle, too.

Principles

I moved a lot
when I was
young & I still
ache a bit at
the thought of
all those
autumns in new
& unfamiliar
landscapes.

Autumns

We had neighbors once who never
cleaned their house & left dishes
in the sink & when there were
no more dishes their dad would
go out & buy another set of
plastic dishes for $9.99 at
Ben Franklin & one winter the
house caught on fire & there
were great piles of melted plastic
everywhere & nothing could be
saved & they moved to a new
town with nothing but the clothes
on their back & a new set of
plastic dishes the church ladies
gave them. Sometimes it
doesn't take much to make a
new start.

New Start

It's a nickel a glass, he
said, because I can't
charge that much since
I ran out of sugar & I
asked if he'd had many
customers & he said
not yet, but he sure
hoped so because he
didn't want to have to
drink the whole thing
himself. It's a refreshing
change, he said, but I
think too much will
make you sick.

Lemonade

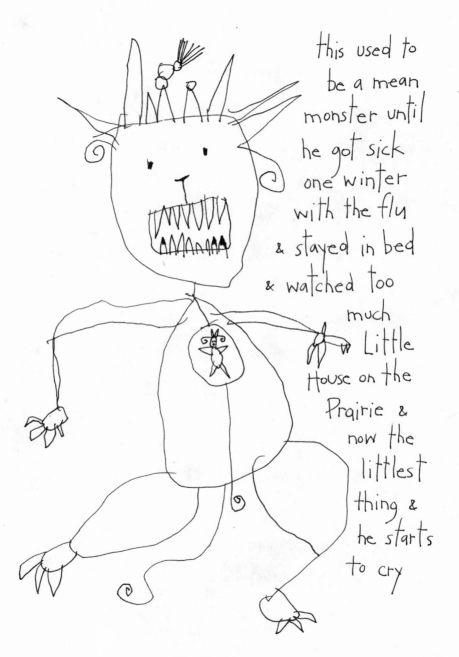

this used to
be a mean
monster until
he got sick
one winter
with the flu
& stayed in bed
& watched too
much Little
House on the
Prairie &
now the
littlest
thing &
he starts
to cry

Little House

If you hold on to the handle, she said, it's easier to maintain the illusion of control. But it's more fun if you just let the wind carry you.

He told me that the
night his mother died,
there were storms &
far away he saw purple
lightning & someone
left the window open
& the room filled
with a swirl of
butterflies & she
slipped out quietly
without anyone noticing

& I'm sure the grief was
softer because of that.

Butterflies

Once upon a time there was a pig
who spoke eight languages & did sculpture
with pieces of wood & rusted metal
he found on his travels. One day
he was out in the woods working
on a new installation piece & he
met a family from a small town
in Tennessee. They had been
walking for days.
   The dad saw the pig & said what
are you doing, little piggie? They
were all quite surprised when the pig said
working with counterbalanced forces
using found objects.
   They all stood around & looked at
the piece for a long time. No one said
anything. Finally, the dad shrugged &
turned to the mom & said I don't know
much about art but I know what I
like & then they killed the pig & ate him.

You can have a plain
hot dog if you want,
he said, but until you've
had a real polish
sausage you're only
half alive. I decided
there were worse things
& I was only ten &
could correct the
serious mistakes later
& the plain dog tasted
just fine, even being
half alive & all.

Half Alive

He wouldn't eat
lobster the first time.
He said it looked too
dangerous & he couldn't
be sure it wasn't watching
from the astral plane or
wherever lobsters went
when they tired of being
food items.

Afterlife

Of course I believe
in heaven, my grandma
used to say.

There's got to be
some reward for
living with your
grandfather all
these years.

Heaven

There are 7 levels of hell, she said,

& I think one of them is reserved for people who bring jello salads to every potluck they go to.

Inferno

Make sure you got
clean underwear, she
always said, in case
you get in an accident
& I always figured
that'd be the least
of my worries, but
now I'm older & I
see there's a lot you
can't control & some
you can control &
clean underwear is
one of those you can.

for the most part

Clean Underwear

When my great-uncle August was in his twenties, he left Iowa & went to study cake decorating at the National Baking Institute in Chicago. He learned everything from spun sugar decorations to ice sculpture.

He went to school for 2 years & when he finished, he went back to Iowa & worked in the family bakery. Except for the odd wedding cake, he never used the fancy stuff he learned. He was in charge of yeast breads & cinnamon rolls.

Just after the end of WWII, the Valley Dairy Farmer's Association had the first of the now famous Milk & Honey Festivals. August made a model of the Statue of Liberty out of 250 pounds of white cheddar cheese, surrounded by American Beauty roses of spun sugar, especially for the occasion.

He showed me the page from Life
magazine he kept folded up in his
wallet, one summer when we visited.
On it was a picture of a much younger
man, smiling next to a 4 foot tall
Liberty. He told me he had 6 proposals
of marriage from that photo, one from
the East Coast even & he smiled &
I saw him grow 30 years younger &
I knew in our hearts we never get old.

I said I
could not
see her
eyes
under her
hat & she
smiled
mysteriously

& said she
liked it
that way.

I remember once I went to
my great-grandmother's house.
It was a big white house & it
always smelled like slightly burned

toast & raspberry jam. She had a
picture of Jesus on the wall in her
living room. She told me his eyes
would follow you around when you
walked. I told a friend about it a
while ago. He nodded & said he used
to have a Chihuahua that did the same
thing.

Her feet moved like small
creatures over the
floor, quiet
& unconcerned
with
anything
but the
business of
dancing.

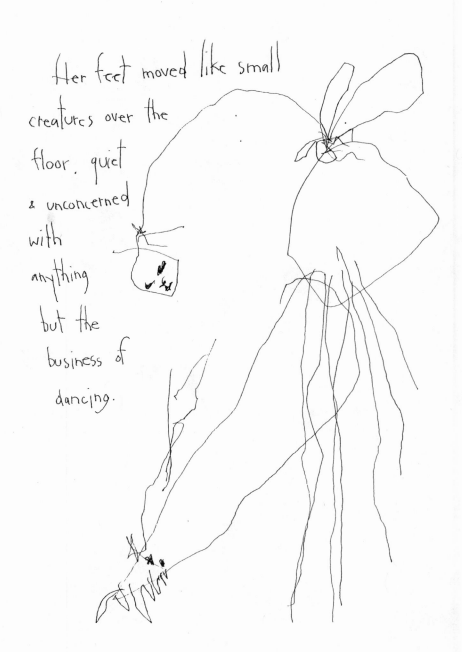

Quiet Dance

One time on Hollywood
Boulevard I saw a young girl
with a baby. It was a crisp
winter morning & her hair
shone dark purple in the sun.
She was panhandling outside
the Holiday Inn & the door
clerk came out & told her
to be on her way & I
remember thinking that
purple seemed like a good
color for a madonna, so
I gave her a dollar just
in case.

Purple Madonna

I don't know if I really believe
in all the saints, she said, but I
pray to them
anyway.

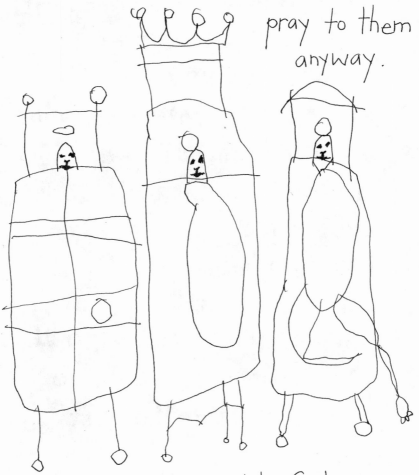

It makes every night feel
more like a slumber party.

Slumber Party

When she wore the hat,
even many years later,
she could always smell
her mother's perfume

& it was hard
to remember
she was
supposed to
be alone.

Scent

After she had
that last big
garage sale
she floated
off into
the sky

& I
heard her
say there was
nothing keeping
her here anymore

& I was much more
cautious about the stuff
I got rid of after that.

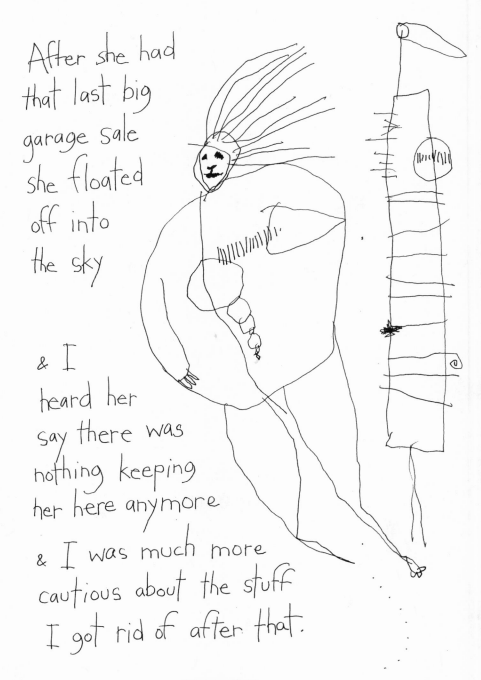

Garage Sale

When I was younger I
used to keep all the stuff
I had in my pockets.
There were a lot of rocks
& little shiny things. As
I got older it got to be
too much to carry & I
couldn't remember why
I kept it anyway so I
finally got rid of it.
Now, I make lists
instead.

I never
trusted
her for a
minute,
she said.
Her purse
was way
too big.

Big Purse

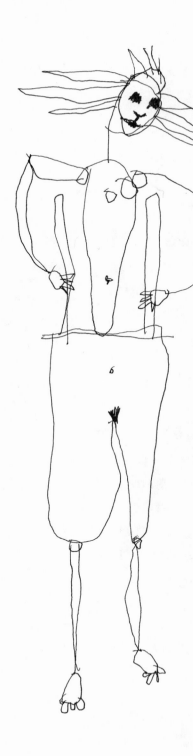

She tried on every
body left but they'd
been pretty well picked
over & all that were
left were a little
worse for wear.
She finally settled
on one that was
pretty good except
for a scuff at the
elbow where you
almost couldn't see
it anyway & as she
walked out into the
world she remembered
thinking next time
I'm going to get here
earlier.

The first time I went to
a fish fry there were all
these rules for surviving
a dinner of catfish like
picking all the bones out &
having soft white bread
in case you did swallow
a bone & chewing until
each bite was soft enough
to squirt through your
teeth & someone said this
was the way the pioneers
used to eat & I thought
no wonder they didn't
live so long back then.

Fish Fry

Early on, I resigned myself
to being in the dark
on all but the
most important
things,
she
said,

& it's not such a bad thing
because you don't see a lot of
the stuff you usually get anxious about.

every time I
looked at the
picture I
thought how I
should have
kissed her, so
finally I hid it
in the attic

& I wonder
if it's still there
with us both so
young & her
waiting to be
kissed

One time I was standing on a corner in Chicago
& a man stopped his car & asked for directions to a
place I knew & I said that's too easy, ask me
something harder & he yelled & said he wasn't
playing games kid & then he drove off

& I think about him sometimes

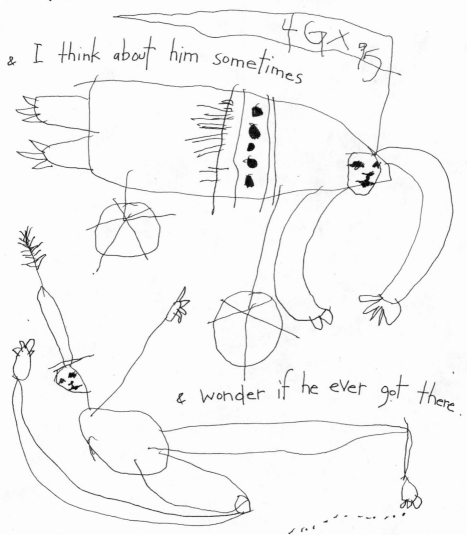

& wonder if he ever got there.

I asked her why

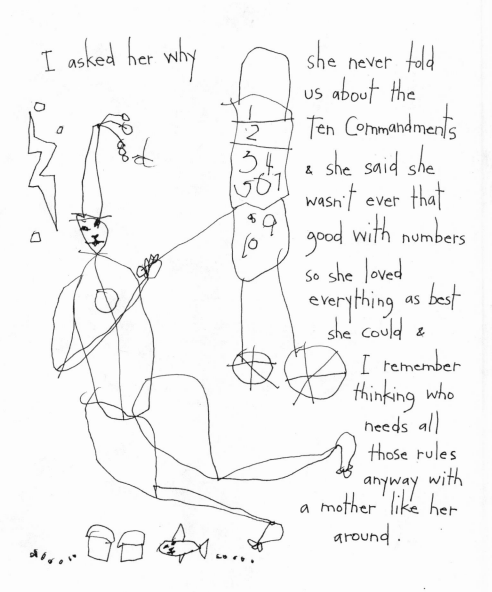

she never told
us about the
Ten Commandments
& she said she
wasn't ever that
good with numbers
so she loved
everything as best
she could &
I remember
thinking who
needs all
those rules
anyway with
a mother like her
around.

Ten Commandments

Older doesn't
always mean
wiser, my
grandfather
once said.
Sometimes
it just means
older.

Wisdom

My grandpa used to tell
us about a man who had
3 heads who lived in his
town & he was always in
the kitchen frying something
or other & even though it
smelled like chicken it was
really the bones of children.
He was awake every time
I saw him, my grandpa
said, even late at night &
we decided maybe he had
3 or 4 jobs but that's what
you need with so many
mouths to feed & then
my grandma would make us
come in & watch educational .
television for our own good .

Front Porch

I tried for a whole summer
to teach our cat to play
the piano. We started with
an easy song. It was 3
Blind Mice. My dad said
it didn't work because
the cat had a tin ear, but
I think it was because she
kept looking around for
the blind mice the whole
time & never gave it her
full attention.

When we visited my grandma in the summer, we'd sit on the porch & watch the moon every night to be sure it made it safely home. My grandma said we should say prayers that it find fulfilling work during the day. It's not like there's a lot of jobs out there for a moon, she said. She had been through the Depression & thought about a lot of things like that.

Work Ethic

It's not so
bad if you
don't think
of it as pizza,
she said. Just
think of it as
another one of
Mom's scary
hot dishes.

Hot Dish

my aunt
had a poodle
she dressed
in little red
sweaters with
little dangly
ball things

& I don't think it was any wonder that
dog was so vicious.

Attack Dog

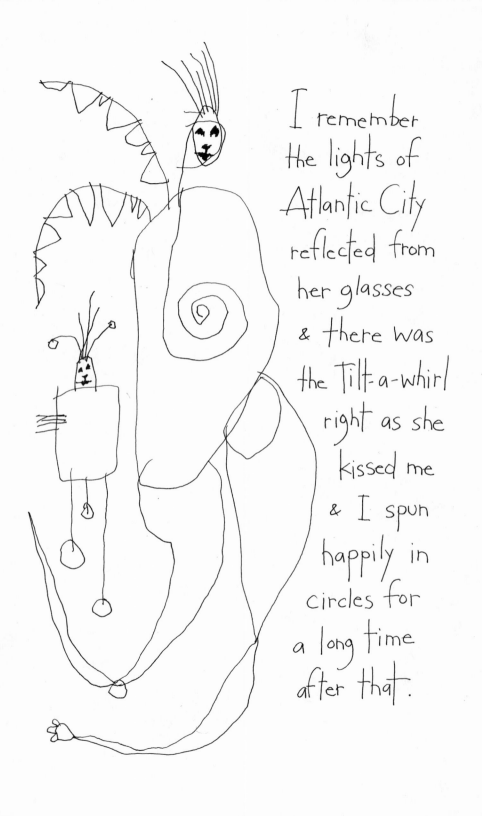

I remember
the lights of
Atlantic City
reflected from
her glasses
& there was
the Tilt-a-whirl
right as she
kissed me
& I spun
happily in
circles for
a long time
after that.

I'd probably have more trouble with the ghosts of the past, she said, if my memory wasn't shot to hell.

I have a friend
who used to ride
bareback in a
circus. In one
picture I've seen
she is wearing
blue sequins with
her smile spread
wide as her arms.
One time I asked
her was it hard to
balance? No, she
said, you always
balance. Only
sometimes, she
added, you balance
on your butt.

this is a
modern dance
with real
animals.
It's supposed
to symbolize
peaceful
coexistence,   but it's usually
pretty loud   & the dancers
have to   watch where they   step
all the time.   I heard someone say they didn't
know peace was so smelly.

I made a bed of nails
once like they do in
India, but my mom
said I'd need my

tetanus
shots first

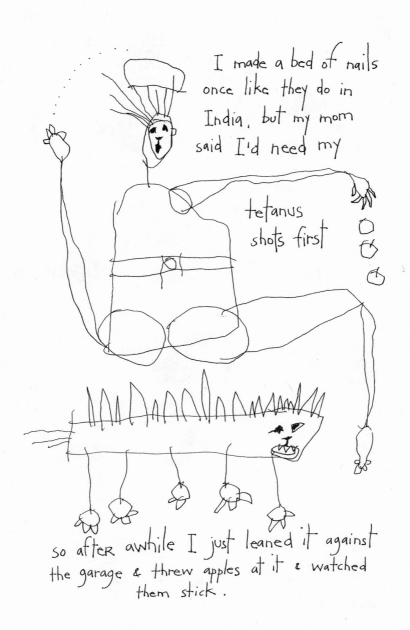

so after awhile I just leaned it against
the garage & threw apples at it & watched
them stick.

Bed of Nails

When we lived
in the city we
used to leave
the lights on
to keep
away the
burglars.

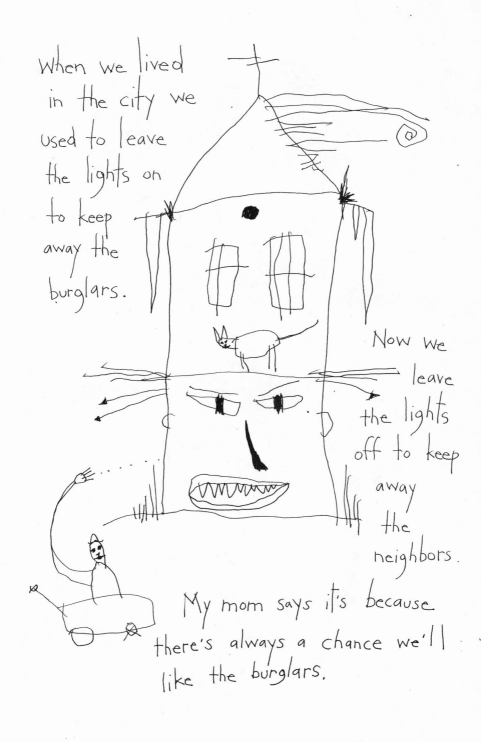

Now we
leave
the lights
off to keep
away
the
neighbors.

My mom says it's because
there's always a chance we'll
like the burglars.

The elephant head
was the most unusual
piece in her wardrobe
& even though she
never wore it in
public, it gave her
great comfort to
know she could if
she wanted to.

she always
camouflaged
herself as
a crowd.

I've never
been lonely,
she said,
but sometimes
it's hard to
think above
the noise.

Crowd

I don't
mind being
a temp,
she told me.

It reminds
me of my
priorities.

Temp

About the Artist

Brian Andreas is an artist, sculptor, and storyteller, who works with new forms of human community. He uses traditional media from fine art, theatre and storytelling, as well as the latest electronic technologies of computer networks, virtual reality and multimedia. His work is shown and collected internationally.

Born in 1956 in Iowa City, Iowa, he holds a B.A. from Luther College in Decorah, Iowa, and an M.F.A. in Fiber and Mixed Media from John F. Kennedy University in Orinda, California.

After years of adventure on the West Coast, he now lives with his wife, Ellen Rockne, and their two wild and beautiful boys in Decorah, Iowa, where he continues to make new stories, and contemplates life from a quieter, colder spot.

About StoryPeople

StoryPeople are wood sculptures, three to four feet tall, in a roughly human form. They can be as varied as a simple cutout figure, or an assemblage of found and scrap wood, or an intricate, roughly made treasure box. Each piece uses only recycled barn and fence wood from old homesteads in the northeast Iowa area. Adding to their individual quirkiness are scraps of old barn tin and twists of wire. They are painted with bright colors and hand-stamped a letter at a time (using the same stamp set that you see on the hand-stamped pages of this book), with original stories. The most striking aspect of StoryPeople are the shaded spirit faces. These faces are softly blended into the wood surface, and make each StoryPerson come alive.

Every figure is marked and numbered at the studio, and is unique because of the materials used. The figures, the colorful story prints, and the books, are available in galleries and stores throughout the US, Canada and the UK (along with a few others scattered about the world), and on our web site. Please feel free to call or write for more information, or drop in on the web at **www.storypeople.com**

StoryPeople
P.O. Box 7
Decorah, IA 52101
USA

800.476.7178
563.382.8060
563.382.0263 FAX

orders@storypeople.com